SMALL GODS OF GRIEF

Also by Laure-Anne Bosselaar:

The Hour Between Dog and Wolf

Night Out: Poems about Hotels, Motels,
Restaurants and Bars
(co-edited with Kurt Brown)

Outsiders: Poems about Rebels, Exiles, and Renegades

Urban Nature: Poems about Wildlife in the City

Small Gods
of Grief

POEMS BY

Laure-Anne Bosselaar

American Poets Continuum Series No. 67

BOA Editions, Ltd. ❦ Rochester, NY ❦ 2001

Manufactured in the United States of America

First Edition

01 02 03 04 7 6 5 4 3 2 1

Publications by BOA Editions, Ltd. — a not-for-profit corporation under section 501 (c) (3) of the United States Internal Revenue Code — are made possible with the assistance of grants from the Literature Program of the New York State Council on the Arts, the Literature Program of the National Endowment for the Arts, the Sonia Raiziss Giop Charitable Foundation, The Halcyon Hill Foundation, The Chase Manhattan Foundation, as well as from the Mary S. Mulligan Charitable Trust, the County of Monroe, NY, and The CIRE Foundation.

See page 86 for special individual acknowledgments.

Cover Design: Geri McCormick

Art: *La digue* by Leon Spilliart,
courtesy Musees Royaux des Beaux-Arts de Belgique

Interior design and composition: Valerie Brewster, Scribe Typography

Manufacturing: McNaughton & Gunn, Lithographers

BOA Logo: Mirko

LIBRARY OF CONGRESS CATALOGING-IN-PUBLICATION DATA

Bosselaar, Laure-Anne, 1943–
Small gods of grief: poems / by Laure-Anne Bosselaar.
p. cm. — (American poets continuum series; no 67)
ISBN 1-929918-05-4 (alk. paper) — ISBN 978-1-929918-06-5 (pbk: alk. paper)
I. Title. II. American poets continuum series; vol. 67.
PS3522.O772 S6 2001
811'.54 — DC21   2001025197

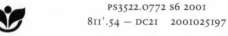

NATIONAL
ENDOWMENT
FOR THE ARTS

State of the Arts

NYSCA

BOA Editions, Ltd.
Steven Huff, Publisher
Richard Garth, Chair, Board of Directors
A. Poulin, Jr., President & Founder (1976–1996)
260 East Avenue, Rochester, NY 14604
www.boaeditions.org

For Mathieu & Sara

One word, and everything is saved,
One word, and all is lost.

ANDRÉ BRETON

CONTENTS

Great Gullet Creek

Great Gullet Creek   5

ॐ

Petition to Be Inconsolable

Petition to Be Inconsolable   13

Our Lady of Pity   15

Follen Street   17

Stamp Box   19

Vase   20

G.O.D.'s Trucks   21

Hope   23

The Pleasures of Hating   24

Harvard Bridge   25

Advice   26

Revisionist Cruelties and Doubts   27

Bench in Aix-en-Provence   29

Listener of Bats   31

Brier   33

Discovering Rhyme   35

Tourists in Brussels   38

Night   41

ॐ

Small Gods of Grief

The Rat Trinity   45

Seven Fragmennts on Hearing a Hammer Pounding   47

Letter to a Friend   53

Dinner at the Who's Who   55

What I feel   57

Next Time   59

Trip   61

Community Garden   62

Night Tide at Ostend   63

For My Son   65

Memory   66

Filthy Savior   67

August City Shadows   69

At Dawn   70

Belong   71

Taller, Wider   73

❦

Notes   75

Acknowledgments   77

About the Author   81

SMALL GODS OF GRIEF

Great
Gullet Creek

Great Gullet Creek

Skies over polders are never empty. They return
to brood here, year after year, the old congruent clouds.

There's no better place on earth to be clouds
than over this wild, windblown edge of Flanders:

no place where rain falls hard as willow knots,
dull as North Sea froth, or with that shade of cobblestone gray —

and nowhere do winds whistle this way: peaked and forlorn
like muskrat calls in *De Grote Geule,* Great Gullet Creek.

Once, in a Brueghel winter, a farmer and I sailed across
Great Gullet Creek — on the anger of Flemish winds.

⚘

Christmas break, 1949. I'm six.
My parents leave me at the *Grote Geule* farm:
they're going on a trip to *very-far-away* again,
the farmers will take care of me — I must be
obedient, and polite.

One day, the oldest farmer packs
clothes, food, and candles in a large basket.
We'll spend a night in the fisherman's cabin
on the creek: *A surprise tomorrow,* he says.
All night gales pound at the walls and windows.

When I wake it's still dark. I watch
the farmer light the oil-lamp, dress over his striped
pajamas, pull a small cross from his vest, kiss it,
and put it back. He feeds the stove, throws in
a match and — *whomp!* —

    flames burst out, spiked and golden,
the farmer's face glows, long shadows waltz
on walls, eel-nets swirl, rods and reels wave,
frozen windowpanes glitter, the floor is liquid,
then — *clang!* — he slams the stove shut,

    and everything is small and cold again.
We stand by the stove, he helps me cover
my chest and back with sheets of brown
paper we waxed the night before — melting
candles in a tin can, then pouring two layers

    on each sheet: *Wind-rage armors*
he says, handing me blue varnished wooden
shoes. On the table, lit by the oil-lamp,
two twigs of licorice wood, a rock of raw sugar,
an orange, two chunks of black bread.

    He cuts the orange in two, shatters
the rock with his knife, and stuffs the pieces
deep into the orange halves. I chew the sour
bread, suck at the sweet fruit. Outside, cold
light oozes through clouds: daybreak.

❦

Scarves, cowls, coats, gloves. We slip
the licorice twigs in our pockets. Warm
our hands one last time by the stove, open
the door to a wind sharp as nettles.
Door-latch. Gate. Gate-latch.

We walk toward the frozen creek,
he pisses long and steamy on a mooring pole.
Behind the poplars a small sun barely
sifts through clouds. A brown buzzard
cowers in a willow like a quilled Quasimodo.

Flat-bottomed and upside-down,
a rowboat lies in the frozen field. The farmer
slips his hand under the prow, orders *Close
your eyes,* then *Look!* Four steel blades dangle
from leather straps: skates! We're going

skating! We sit on the boat's hull, he
ties the skates to our wooden shoes. The wind
slaps down smoke from the cabin's chimney.
Acrid ribbons of coal fumes tangle with reeds.
From across the creek come broken,

wind-gutted calls of village church
bells, *d-dong... d-dong...* He looks at the sky:
*Skating will be good, the wind's angry —
it's coming from Germany.* We set foot
on ice, January chews my cheeks,

but I don't utter a sound: he'd
warned me *Only city fillies fuss.* He hunches
like a buzzard before taking flight, grabs

the sides of his coat, opens his arms
wide, turns his back to the wind, lets it

belt against him — propel him:
he orders *Crouch, grab my coat,*
hold on! A gust whacks me against him,
he takes two wide strides, pulls me along:
the wind pushes us, we're sailing!

The ice is littered with leaves, twigs,
my skates send thunder through my legs,
I can barely breathe. My lips and throat
hurt, but I scream *Faster, faster!* He straightens
his huge back, opens his arms

even wider, his skates clatter,
pelt my face with ice, we're picking up
speed, the creek sounds like a hundred drums,
my eyes freeze, I can no longer see, but I'm
no city filly, no city filly.

☙

When we reach the opposite bank,
our faces are blue, knees so stiff we can't
straighten our legs. I'm thirsty, he gives me
his licorice stick to chew, rubs his palms,
blows into them, and puts them to my cheeks.

Winter blows low oboe notes
through the reeds. A few yards away,
northern shovelers quack and ruffle

their feathers, sending rust and cobalt
flashes over the ice.

We untie our skates, turn our backs
to the creek, and walk through the potato
polders toward the village of Kieldrecht.
My wooden shoes slip on frozen loam,
I trip, he holds me by the wrist.

The winds won't stop, they churn
clouds, send them crashing into the steel
blade of the horizon. We don't speak,
hurry through the village toward the café
by the windmill.

He pushes open the heavy oak door.
A few nods and taciturn *daag* from stout
drinking men. We head for the high
delft-tiled stove, hang our coats on a chair
beside it. The tables

are covered with thick, ruglike
tapestries, I rub my hands over their wool:
they smell of must and winter, like the hem
of the farmer's coat. He orders Dutch gin,
buttered bread, mugs of broth.

He pours gin in my mug. We slurp
and slurp. He throws back his head, closes
his eyes, crosses his hands on his belly,
smiles. Behind heavy lace curtains, I watch
clouds shred against the church steeple.

On the way back, our skates
ring as he slings them over his shoulder.
Winds blow night deep into the streets
of Kieldrecht. Bundled silhouettes slip
out of low doors, lock shutters,

disappear. Bent figures hurry by
on black, high-handled bicycles: *Good-night
farmer,* they say, *Good-night farmer,* he answers.
We hurry home through the potato polders.
When we near the farm, the dog yaps,

cows bellow in the barn. At dinner,
I ask the farmer for the cross he hid in his vest.
I kiss it, so it will keep my parents *very-far-
away.* Outside, the Flemish winds sing.
From the village steeple fall six low notes.

Petition to
Be Inconsolable

Petition to Be Inconsolable

Listen to this: *rationalism* —
what an ugly word, heady with the sagacious
rational, insufferably suffixed with *ism.*

I ban it from my vocabulary,
from the only thesaurus I trust:
the abridged one I protect when I make

a fist against my chest, the same fist
I brandish to the fourteen slats of the blinds
I slammed down just now

to stop staring at that immutable
mountain in which I know how to find
consolation, but don't want to tonight.

I petition to be inconsolable
for today's fourteen sorrows — one per slat:

for a cloud at dawn tearing its heart out
trying to obscure the sun;

for that beech branch on Spring Street
whipped to shreds by each passing truck;

for the gardens I planted, then left;

for the photograph of my dead friend
buckling more each day on the fridge door;

for the three times I stumbled today,

for my lubberly body,

the shame of it;

for the fist *inside* my chest

and for raising it, still, against my father;

for his shame of me,

for the shame of him
in me;

for spurning consolation
with fourteen slammed slats;

for another day of dying

and for welcoming this—against all reason.

Our Lady of Pity

It's only 4:10 in an afternoon
of cars, trucks, and school buses ahead
and behind me, freeing the same kids
they locked in hours ago — thousands —

who all said *I, me, yes,* or *no* at least
ten times today, who came from or went to
somewhere, who listened, or didn't,
like everyone did or didn't during this day

of backed-up cars, subways,
houses, each with its doors and windows —
think of this — each with windows or doors
that were opened, locked, or left behind

for other doors, other windows;
and it's only 4:10 in an afternoon of people
who never had a choice of which color eyes
they'd have to look through

for the rest of their lives
or in which arms, sea, bar, year they'll die
without ever having held that man
or that woman they saw once —

a scorching they'll never forget —
that one life that could have changed theirs
forever, could have damned or saved them:
all those women and men, from *this* life,

the life they're stuck with at 4:10 today,
some of them idling with me on the corner
of Rindge and Rice, and it's not even raining,
not even cold or beautiful,

and now my gray Toyota is jammed
between a yellow bus and a blue pickup,
while this guy croaks *Car Sales*
on the radio as I stare at a church sign

begging: *Pray to Our Lady of Pity* —
Pray? For pity? Me? For what? —
It's too late in the day to pray for that:
there's nothing left to redeem,

and I won't need the Lady's
pity when I'll be mass-transited
to the clogged soul-jam up there, stuck
again — but among

the meek and some Popes, and
waiting, waiting for the dog, our friends,
my husband, our kids, then finally
for a God, *any* God who'll

take me, who'll say it was okay
not to pray for the end of this day,
at the beginning of this millennium, crisp,
bewildered, and destined.

Follen Street

I do it each time we move, do it
again to our new house in this listless
Cambridge street:

press my forehead and palms
to the door, ask *Forgive me* before
I bring in my mess: relics,

hopes, insomnia, clocks.
Then, while the man I love carefully
prints our names on the mailbox,

I chase vacancy away with broom
and books, hang the paintings — those fake
windows I need

to comfort me from what I keep
seeing through lucid ones: the same skies,
traffic, worn-out dogs,

and always, everywhere, an old
widow or widower trying to be dapper,
the woman with dust

on her nice little hat and too much
blush; the man in his brown shoes,
and gray pants an inch

too short: it gets me each
time, that whole inch missing. And oh,
what they carry:

his briefcase flat, flagrantly
useless, but something to hold on to —
her bag clasped around

her "just-in-cases" she never
leaves without: so much like what I
bring to this house — things, things

to hold on to in case night
freezes the shutters closed and only
my name remains on the mailbox.

Stamp Box

Stuck shut for years
on Father's desk before he died,

stuck shut on mine since.
Ugly, useless, dumb. But if I

throw it away I'll keep
seeing it gone: something

missing I'd miss dusting.
So I'll keep this damn black

Bakelite box Father loved.
We do that, don't we?

Place a picture here,
a relic there, taking them along,

house in, life out—
passing the dusting on,

father to daughter,
mother to son.

Vase

For years
in our old
house it stood
amid our books
and in the way. It's in
the way again — here on
my desk — stopping my gaze
between a page and a daydream.
I love the tacky landscape on its belly:
trees, meadows, and a green hollow where
a river sings. Then there's Art, fishing the same
bend for years now, under the tallest tree, its crown
cresting up the vase's neck, almost growing out of it. I've
named him Art for Arthur Rimbaud, although no one called
him Art then, not his pale, pious sister, not his manic mother
who shrieked out each letter of his name while she whipped
him; not even old, needy Verlaine. (Oh, behind the closed
curtains of his room, the lust in the lines he whispered
to magazine pages, slick with wild Spanish dancers
and laughing Italians!) But the Rimbaud on this
vase is long past that. He's turned his back
on the world: fishing without bait in a
glass river, longing for drunken
boats to take him back to
Savannas, forests,
shores, and suns!

G.O.D.'s Trucks

I'm not making this up
    — they bolt through
    traffic all year long —
"G.O.D." plastered in black

on their fronts, sides, backs,
    — letters spaced by periods
    big as brake drums —
on rigs roaring all over town, for

Guaranteed Overnight Delivery.

Six- to eighteen-wheelers
    — Volvo engines,
    Bendix brakes —
dispatched across New England's

gritty roads and city grids
    — loading kayaks, anoraks,
    porn, or petunias —
kept track of on G.O.D.'s ledger for:

Overnight Delivery — *guaranteed.*

Why didn't I think of it before
    — it's been in my face
    all this time for Christ's sake —
their 800 number the one to call:

no more shrinks, no novenas
   — rosaries clicking
      like phones hanging up —
I'll call them for a date with

Guaranteed Overnight Delivery's

roving rep, show him my load
     — how it piles up, weighs,
     chokes up my days —
sign a contract, swear I'll pay

overtime, taxes, tonnage and tips
     — *anything you*
     charge, sir, is okay —
I'll pay. But take it away:

Deliver me. Overnight. Guarantee it.

Hope

I hadn't hoped this far:
that I could be writing this

today — now. I type
"now" and see tomorrow

in red on the calendar:
Veterans Day.

The Pleasures of Hating

I hate Mozart. Hate him with that healthy
pleasure one feels when exasperation has

crescendoed, when lungs, heart, throat,
and voice explode at once: *I hate that!* —

there's bliss in this, rapture. My shrink
tried to disabuse me, convinced I use Amadeus

as a prop: *Think further, your father perhaps?*
I won't go back, think of the shrink

with a powdered wig, pinched lips, mole:
a transference, he'd say, *a relapse*: so be it.

I hate broccoli, chain saws, patchouli, bra-
clasps that draw dents in your back, roadblocks,

men in black kneesocks, sandals and shorts —
I *love* hating that. Loathe stickers on tomatoes,

jerky, deconstruction, nazis, doilies. I delight
in detesting. And love loving so much after that.

Harvard Bridge

This is the day's last offering: the sky bleeds
    like a sacrificial lamb, the sun's wine-bloated host
        slides deep into dusk's throat.

Crimson floods the Charles, banks and reeds blush:
    roofs, cars, puddles, and boats are aflame;
        every one, each thing is soaked red —

but no one seems to notice the sun
    drowning in the river like the spent fist
        of a sinking God. I'm in my car, foolishly

trying to make eye contact with someone — *Isn't this*
    amazing? — as cars pass me left and right,
        honking, angry, in a hurry to get

somewhere. What can I do but follow —
    brake, blink, bleat with the chorus,
        losing my smile as I join this exodus

toward night, while Dylan nasals on the radio:
    ring them bells with an iron hand
        so the people will know —

as the sky fades to rust, and stoplights
    flash, and a kid in a cap whacks
        at trash cans with his baseball bat.

Advice

Don't show
your work
until you're
ready to
defend it.

Then, let
others
call it art.

Revisionist Cruelties and Doubts

When I click on *Empty
Trash,* the can icon on my screen
makes a cute crash sound,

the lid flicks up, the can
snaps shut, and the room hums again
with my Mac's windy whir.

Done. Gone. What I just
wrote — zapped. No regrets.
No bending down under the desk,

to salvage and palm-flatten
scribbled eight-and-a-half-
by-eleven paper balls.

Censured, the lovely lines
the stuttering fricatives of fallen leaves,
or *long and melancholic*

*shadows linger in the village
square at dusk.* Click, drag, trash,
quit. Kill those little darlings

electronically. No wasted
trees, lead, ink, or proofreader marks
on paper doomed

to burn with corncobs
and clams on a dump stuttering out
useless heat. But

what if? What if that heat,
one long and melancholic dusk,
warmed a gull's frozen wings?

Or muses pilfered dumps,
rescued lines and brought them
back to us purified?

What if computer trash-
can contents composted in there
and came bursting

out one day — a thick, garbled
muck — and censored our writings
with binary bedlam?

Better stick to paper baskets,
pads, pencils, pens. Better fuel
the dumps with scribblings;

write by hand about those gulls —
the tattered pages of their wings
uncensored in the wind.

Bench in Aix-en-Provence

There they are again, the lovers
    — midthirties, colorless
      clothes, hair, hands —
having their lunch-break

on the same beige bench
    — in the jabbering street,
      pigeons nodding at their feet —
under a paltry plane tree.

They simply sit there, not saying a word.

For days now, I've watched them
    — from a narrow window
      on the Rue Marceau —
place a single napkin on their knees,

a coffee cup on her side, a beer can on his
    — each at the exact same
      distance from their hips —
and don't drink or eat,

but simply sit there, not saying a word.

There is such resilience in how they sit
    — hands, knees, feet
      together, neatly —
in the way they stare at the pigeons,

or at the clouds moving in like frayed sheets
    — and smile at the same things
    at the same time —
that I know they haven't had it yet, sex.

They simply sit there, not saying a word.

And I find myself hoping
    — as I close the window
    on them, on noon, on Aix —
that they'll wait before spending

their lunch-break having it: sex
    — calling it *making love* but too soon
    calling it anything but that —
instead of coming back to their bench at noon,

to simply sit there, not saying a word.

Listener of Bats

There. I watched it once again
     — at 4:15 today,
      on the last day in May —
sunrise. Day's sudden juncture

so predictable: what is lit first —
     and always the longest:
      skies, steeples, roofs —
and what will be lit at midday only,

when all shadows, for an instant, recoil.

Bittersweet hour, dawn
     — for the listeners of bats,
      shufflers of night —
when darkness pulls back, yes,

but light comes too fast, then arcs
     — with day's bane
      of locusts, traffic, rain —
flares down everything,

and all shadows stretch, then recoil.

At dawn, may I die
     — during those mingling,
      willing hours —
when colors are tender

and lazily blend
        — when waves braid
        their light in the sea —
and there is time before

all shadows, for an instant, recoil.

I'll leave slight as a bat's whir
        — when night recants
        but day is not ablaze —
and before the cicadas

jab their relentless jeers
        — *cheater, cheater*
        cheat, cheat —
That's when I'll go, at dawn. Silent, slow:

the way a shadow recoils.

Brier

A friend betrayed me yesterday.
I loved him for his hungers

and awkward flat feet
he stomped as if he wanted to leave

a mark everywhere he went.
I never told him how that stomping

moved me, the same sad way
this clumsy brier does,

waving, trying to be noticed
in the dust of a Boston off-ramp.

My friend betrayed me
for a fast mark, a few gasps around

a spilled secret no bigger
than a brier's thorn.

I'm in one of the cars the off-
ramp jams into town, and because

it would cause horn-blasting
rage, and because for each betrayal

we lose a little fervor, I don't
step out to tear a leaf

from the brier to keep.
Lost secrets, friends, lost fervors:

we are made of this dust.
Let briers grow from it, and bloom.

Discovering Rhyme

They came cheap, the *Petites Punitions*
nuns flung at us for minor sins — dyslexic
signs of the cross, missed

confessions, whispers during Silence —
Punishments fell: copy two, ten, twenty
Lord's Prayers or Hail Marys

on calligraphy paper, cursives
correctly curled, capitals clinging to margins,
black ink for consonants, vowels in red.

The wars I waged in those French
syllables — wanting love-red vowels to win
over habit-black consonants!

I hated hailing Mary, for anything
full of grace shamed me: I was homely,
lumpy, and had never been baptized —

three reasons for perpetual doom:
no sips of our Savior's red liquor for me,
or tastes of His wan

flesh on my tongue. Banished,
I spent mass in the chapel's back pews,
bored, counting red stained-

glass pieces over blue, gold
versus green in the west window
where Mary Magdalene

held Christ's foot to her breast
so tenderly. On drizzly days, slow
raindrops sobbed down

Christ's flank unto her longing
face — I loved watching how nothing
distracted her from looking up at Him,

how she let Him quench His gaze
into hers. It was on one of those days
that novices sang a new hymn.

Its melody was rueful, flowed
with long *ooo* sounds: two words,
amour and *toujours*

soared in unison — it was
new to me: music inside a song, words
poured melody *into* a tune —

swooned in harmony like Christ
and Mary Magdalene. I hadn't heard this
as achingly before.

After that day, I slipped rhymes
in each line of my small punishments:
Hail frail Mary,

blessed art *thou now* — the sounds
crimson with *amour* — rhyme my song
pour toujours.

Tourists in Brussels

Brussels beats with rain-soaked
drums, Flemish and French pound
in Holy Processions by the Brewer's
Guild Hall,

    streets and alleys ooze with history:
this is the town that ballasts my accent,
here's the city you wanted to see.
So I show you the sidewalk

    where Verlaine shot Rimbaud,
gargoyles grimacing from gables,
church fronts niched with virgins
and saints,

    a café where Baudelaire drank
absinthe and Trappist Monk stouts.
But we're both lost in this tangle of masks,
smells, tastes and sounds —

    why go further into the past,
why tell you we're only blocks away
from the place that still splinters
my voice?

    I won't show you where nuns
taught me to be silent in Flemish or French,
and repent in Latin for sins I made up
to have something to say, then

regret in the rank deceptions
of Catholic confessionals. While you study
the past in the pages of a guidebook, everything
I learned, all I

see, is muted by my being nine here,
nine thousand silences ago, when I
returned to the convent from a family
reunion, raped —

the blood held up inside me
with a piece of my panties torn off —
but by me this time — in the toilet
of a Brussels-bound train.

I could speak of Sin now, knew
a Mortal one I could regret — but a new
silence had been forced into me: *Nothing
Happened, You Hear?*

said my cousins Michel and Paul,
and the woman, Nicole. So I stepped
off the train, asked the gargoyles
to curse them, *Michel, Paul,*

and the woman, Nicole, searched
my missal for their saints: *Michel, Paul,
Nicole,* crossed them out — religiously —
each time they appeared and never

spoke their names again. *Nothing
Happened.* But love, if I'm quiet tonight,

it's not with the fear to say *something*
happened,

  but with the peace distance brings,
and the solace of our story: I'm nothing
but a tourist here now, lost in a foreign
city with you,

  knowing I'll soon turn my back
to Brussels, leave its history behind
like tourists do, with the masks of the past
frozen inside our disposable camera.

Night

wakes in bat wings
sinks into darkness
as they do

as they do
night's wings never
cast shadows

Small Gods of Grief

The Rat Trinity

That rat's too smart to come
to the rows of crumbs I sowed
by the pond; he has the patience of true
hunger: he'll wait me out

with the same tenacity
I had as a child, hungry to grow
strong enough to escape the nunnery
without being caught.

I loved the rats of Bruges
I watched from the dorm window,
how they slunk out the courtyard
sewer grill, slid along walls,

slipped down the cellar steps
like whispers, and vanished into gray.
I loved three in particular — christened
them the Trinity:

the Father was slick, sullen,
the Daughter tense but lissome,
and the fat-bellied one, the Holy Ghost,
maker of miracles, was the Mother.

I imagined they came
from Antwerp, from the port's stinking
sewage by the Coal Wharf, last quay
before the wild, eager sea.

And there were times, when
beatings seared my skin with hues
of oil on the river Scheldt, and I
squeezed my thumbs

in my fists through long
convent nights, there were times
I prayed to the Rat Trinity. To
show me the way

out, through Bruges sewers
and cobbled rows, then underground
to Ghent, out again through velour
fields of wheat near Antwerp,

and hasten to my parents'
house where Mother wore silk
and Father blew smoke halos in the air.
I prayed the rats

to bring me back to the young
whispers of their bed and into Mother's
fat, white belly. To crown them
with the trinity

they had hungered for:
a Father, Mother, and from their fusion
not I, but unscorned, chosen: one
divine being—a son.

Seven Fragments on Hearing
a Hammer Pounding

May 31st, 2000

      I sit by a larch, pen and journal
in my lap. Two suns in my tea, the lemon
slice the brightest.

      Tannin clouds the mug's sky,
today's fate still steeps in its leafy depths.
I count each blow of a hammer

      somewhere up the street,
want it to stop after seven, seventeen,
twenty-one,

      anything with a seven,
but it never does, even when I give it
seven last chances. I need

      an augury, a sign to help me
believe that the pounding means something —
something good.

Antwerp, 1947

      My parents, hoarding
profits from what they call
the good war, are happy:

a million hammers, ten million
nails are needed to rebuild Europe,
and my father sells iron and steel.

One's misery is
another's happiness, he says
as we drive through

Pelican Street and what
had been the Jewish Quarter.
I am five.

(Fifty years later I remember winds blew dust and ashes
through the empty bellies of bombed houses. Some walls still
stood. For no one. Gutted doors and windows looked like
screaming mouths caught in brick: blocks of them. And
blocks and blocks of them —)

Father spits out
his cigarette: *Nothing's*
changed here, only pigeons

and rats instead of Jews.
I don't know that word: *joden,*
he says in Dutch, *joden.*

I ask what kind
of animals *joden* are. My parents
laugh, laugh.

(To think I spoke their tongue before finding mine —
O Gods of Grief, grant me this: some tongues will die,
some tongues must.)

Voting Tongue

Yet this Spring of 2000, thirty
percent of the Flemish voted extreme
right. In France,

Austria, Germany, Israel —
Israel, too — votes speak menacing
tongues and millions

pretend they don't hear it. And I
write about a lemon slice in my tea?
About needing a hammer to stop its

blows in groups of seven
because a priest, from behind the barbed
grills of a confessional window

once hissed to me: "You'll be saved
only if seven generations remember you
as a good Christian"?

Write about Your Times

1961. Oscar Vladislas Milosz
teaches writing workshops in Brussels.

I brandish my notebooks filled
with Baudelaire, Aragon, Sartre —

I'm eighteen:

Everything's been said, Monsieur Milosz,
what is left to write about?

Write about your time, he said,
nothing's been said about your time.

Then, on the blackboard:

Le Présent: Lieu seul d'où j'écris: Soleil de la Mémoire
(The Present: single Place from where I write: Memory's Sun).

Two suns in my tea, the lemon slice
the brightest. Today's writing still brews
in a mug's leafy depths.

From which memory
must I — will I — speak?

Which present do I —
must I — call mine?

Give Yourself in Belief

Glued to the pages of my journal, a letter from a friend:

"It is necessary to give yourself in belief to the motivating
event. It is necessary to be gullible. Once that part of the
writing is done, one has to become ruthless. You must become
an expert at the first, before becoming expert at the other,
even if it means writing nothing but junk. At this point in
your writing the process is more important than what is

produced by the process. You need to do more to give yourself
to the emotion, the event, the story."

Memory's Sun: a vote, emotion, belief —

Thief, 1950

Oxblood velvet drapes
frame Father's office windows.
Ten million hammers

pound nails in Belgium
France, Holland, Italy, England,
Russia, Poland,

and Germany — Germany,
too — building roofs, barns, houses,
churches, schools,

railroads, and bridges
after the war. Father loads iron
and steel onto Antwerp's ships —

he's a rich man now.
I wait for him to return
from meetings. I'm seven

A dusk sun strokes
the drapes, his mahogany
desk gleams bloodred.

I open a drawer, see
Father's pen. I hear ships
from the harbor urge me —

Doo-it, dooo — so I
reach for it, gold and heavy,
take and uncap it,

draw a line in my palm —
the ink is green, a strong, hard
green. The door opens,

Father grabs his pen,
slaps my face, knees my chest,
but listen:

my need to write
started then, a hunger to write,
to own a pen

but not, but never —

Summons

Dusk. On a chair by the larch,
my journal and pen.

O small Gods of Grief,
grant me to write from seven memories

deep, but not in my father's
tongue — but never with his pen.

Letter to a Friend

for S.D.

A dank dawn. Sodden light
on damp brick. Lilacs rot to rust,
and the crow's nest barren in the oak.

It's you I long for most today,
to sit across this kitchen table, your
awkward legs

comfortable under it for once,
our inner clamors quiet for this while
of conversation — vague as this day.

Imagine the sound of a marble
bouncing down the stone steps of an empty
house, you said, months ago,

and I've been hearing its
resonance since, a desolate din, chilling
as this kitchen where nothing's

lit and everything seeps
with stillness. It took me
all this time to understand why

that sound haunted me so —
now I need you to take it back: it has
no place here, no reason

to bounce in me any longer.
Come soon. Bang your palm against
the door as you always do: too loud,

as if you wanted to scare silence
out of itself, out of a house in which
no one would be there to listen.

Dinner at the Who's Who

Amid swirling wine
and flickers of silver, guests quote
Dante, Brecht, Kant, and one another.

I wait in the hall after not
powdering my nose, trying to re-
compose that woman who'll

graciously take her place
at the table and won't tell her hosts:
I looked into your bedroom

and closets, smelled your
Obsession and *Brut,* sat on your bed,
imagined you in those

spotless sheets, looked
long into the sad eyes of your son
staring at your walls from a velvet frame,

and I tried to smile at myself
in your mirrors, wondering if you
smile that way too:

those resilient little smiles
one smiles at oneself before facing
the day, or another long

night ahead—guests coming
for dinner. So I wait in this hall because
there are nights it's hard

not to blurt out: Enough!
Stop the *Pulitzer, Wall Street, P.C.,*
Dante, sex, wars, have some Chianti...

let's stop, let's talk—
about our thirsts and obsessions,
bedrooms and closets,

the brutes in our mirrors,
the eyes of our sons. There is time yet—
let's *talk:* I'm starving.

What I feel

as I bend over buckets of super-
market tulips, while I sort through
their scentless clusters, is

shame
for my big hips, those offending
glutei confronting the fashionably slim
women brushing past me on their way in;

annoyance
at my notion that tulips squeak in thanks
when I pull them out of their pail,
or curse me when I squeeze them back in;

envy
for a woman's glorious butt, calves, and carat-
heavy hands on carts brimming with everything
I hate: air-freshener, condoms, and Soy-onnaise;

exasperation
at the yuppie yakking about his wife's lipo-
suction to a friend while the bagger drops
a watermelon on my apricots and eggs; then,

grief
driving home, to see the same bald woman
waving at nobody again from her Sunlight
Nursing Home window;

joy
walloping my chest as I open the door and see
my husband, albeit swearing at the TV,
his fervid face lit by breaking news and wars;

longing
for his hands on me as I watch
them clutch his coffee,

consolation
from our whispers in bed: love's
long rosaries,

and peace
as I fall asleep hungering for more
of these good, tough days.

Next Time

I'll be a cello, rowboat,
bench, snowman, but nothing
alive — no more heft, hope, hunger.

No eyes so shortly fused
to the heart they glut at any goad:
TV ads, mall openings, even

"Over the Rainbow"
violining in elevators. I won't be
a gull, whale, snake. No dolphin,

or rat. Not that. I want
to be a *thing*. Heartless as a parking
meter, tough as a turnstile:

a simple, made thing. An *it*
that knows or fears nothing.
Not even that, at the exact

fraction between day
and night, each thing on earth
does live: statues stretch,

roads buckle, meadows
sneeze, people in photographs
exchanges stories,

and all the carved initials
weep in trees. I can live with that:
it's only an instant.

I'll be a stethoscope or willow.
No, better, a mirror, mere reflector:
bare, blunt, facing an opposite wall,

waiting for someone to look
for me, then *into* me, to check a tooth,
smile, or wrinkle: I'll mirror them

mercilessly. But not for you.
Remember this: find me among the other
mirrors, come stand between that wall

and me, and watch, watch
closely: for you I'll lie — show you
only what you hope to see.

Trip

She sees him waving
in her back-view mirror,

waves back. Each time,
each time, she prays

it won't be the last.
When she returns,

she's furious
at his mess, and pouts.

Community Garden

I watch the man bend over his patch,
a fat gunnysack at his feet. He combs the earth

with his fingers, picks up pebbles around
tiny heads of sorrel. Clouds bruise in, clog the sky,

the first hard drops pockmark the dust,
then it pours. The man wipes his hands on his chest,

opens the sack, pulls out top-halves
of broken bottles, and plants them, firmly,

over each head of sorrel — tilting the necks
toward the rain. His back is drenched, so am I,

his careful gestures clench my throat,
wrench a hunger out of me I don't understand,

can't turn away from. The last plant
sheltered, the man straightens his back,

swings the sack over his shoulder, looks
at the sky, then at me and — as if to end

a conversation — says: *I know they'd
survive without the bottles, I know. But less. Less*

well. He leaves the garden, blurs away. I hear
myself say it to no one: I never had a father.

Night Tide at Ostend

Hours ebb. The horizon
sags into sea. Not much left of day:
towels that checkered the beach

folded away. No children
tumbling from castles like pawns. Last
walkers leave: a man and his mutts,

the woman who clutched
her shoes to her chest for hours —
all chased away by the night tide exhaling

Huh-shhh... Huh-shhh.
I walk the line of darkening surf,
watch waves push closer, closer,

but toward what? A deserted
shore scarred with scraps that will not
drown: driftwood, plastic.

I used to think those waves
were herds of horses, manes
frothing, hundreds of ocean

hooves thundering toward
land: *this* land their destination,
these wild satin shores —

not just a jagged tidemark
swallowed by sand. I loved how
each swell lunged, surged,

     charged to shore — but they
don't — it takes three: two waves heave,
curl, but drown into a third,

     and that one alone makes it,
marking its reach with nothing but rags,
sticks, some shredded rope.

     Let gulls peck at that:
they're experts at what to filch,
what to leave behind. I'll leave

     empty-handed: no longer
need the North Sea's relics.
Behind me, erratic tracks —

     my footmarks: let the night
tide efface them while beacons
light the bones of a distant harbor.

For My Son

I sit against the scarred trunk of an oak.
The sun barely winnows through its branches.

Beyond a lit spot small as a newborn's fist,
a twig quivers, then arcs toward light.

What caused such languid inclination
makes its way down the leaf: a tiny snail,

gold as corn. For an instant, they sway,
lit, in utter balance — then, in a deep bow,

the leaf releases its weight onto earth and curls
back into the shade — the vitreous path

of that moment now in its center. Mathieu,
if nature's cruelties know no limits,

neither do the boundaries of its grace.
I give thanks for you.

Memory

What wouldn't
I do to have

the kindest place
in yours.

Filthy Savior

Look at this storm, the idiot:
it pours its heart out *here,* of all places,
an industrial suburb on a Sunday,

drenches cinder-blocks
and parking lots, wastes its gusts
on smokeless stacks,

not even a trash can to send
rumbling through streets. And lightning —
forking itself to death to hit

nothing, what a waste. What if
I hadn't been here, lost too? Four a.m.,
and I'm driving to nowhere again,

a shirt over my nightgown,
reciting Rimbaud aloud, like an insomniac
idiot — scared to death

by my longing for it, death,
so early in the morning, and driving
until the longing runs on empty.

The windshield wipers can't
keep up with this deluge, and I almost
run over a flapping white

thing in the middle of the street. I step
out, it's a gull, one leg caught in a red
plastic net snared around its neck.

I throw my shirt over the shrieking
thing, take it to the car, search my bag
for something, anything,

find a nail file to saw at the net.
The gull is huge, filthy, shits and pecks.
I slip a sleeve over its head:

you idiot, I'm trying to save you —
hold it down, cut, pull, free the leg,
neck, hold the gull against me,

fighting for its life, its crazed
heart beats against mine. I step out,
open the shirt — and there it goes —

letting the wind pluck it
away, suck it into a cloud and it's
gone — like some vague,

bleak longing —
as the rain lifts and the suburbs
emerge in dirty white light.

August City Shadows

Sun-flung, wall-tossed,
skyscraper-cast.

Alley-narrow, avenue-
vast. Heat shelters,

light ogres: here's to urban
shades so tranquil, so dark,

I can kneel inside them
and be shadowless at last.

At Dawn

Crows — their constant
beak-clicking, triple-beat squawks.

My love as he sighs, stirs,
weighs a wrist or knee on me,

then sinks back, coiled
into the thick flesh of sleep.

The coffeemaker's chokes,
the garbage truck's brake-squeaks.

Last night's sweet crumbs
of dried-out apricot pie.

Then — light: how it creeps
down night's taut rope, lands,

aslant, on the kitchen counter
to shellac two clementines

shrinking in a chipped bowl.
I take note, write it down: crows' scorn,

love's weight, street sounds —
tastes, colors, death, charms

crammed into a fraction of dawn:
all of this — already gone.

Belong

for Kurt

Here are boughs snow broke
from our birch, metal-blue berries
bending a twig, two frozen buds:

for you — take them, my hands
are cold, I worked in the yard too long,
wearing the brown

shoes you left by the shed.
The word *belong* hummed in my head,
and — while crows screeched and police

cars keened through dawn —
I cleared our garden of winter's waste:
all those broken limbs to gather,

they didn't hang on, *belong*
any longer. What a word: the heft in it,
dare and weight. It defies: *Hold on,*

belong, and *be — for long.*
So let's keep this ugly bunch, like I
kept that shred of stained window

blown apart in the convent chapel —
Sister Kelleen gone mad again, lighting
all the candles she could find,

heaping chairs loaded with her flames
all the way up to St. Bosco's face,
longing to see him lit, be-

longing to her as she stacked
her scaffold up to his chin, broke
candles in two for more fire until it

scorched his throat, reached his locked
face, and she saw his gaze soften. That's when
the music started — faint,

glassy notes, *ping, ding, ping:*
the window behind Bosco split with heat,
and burst, sucking in snow — heavy,

dousing snow — the sudden draft
collapsing him to the floor. Kelleen
screamed his name through the halls,

then walls, when they locked
her up again. Then it stopped. They said
she'd snapped, was taken

away, she didn't *belong.*
That's when I understood what that word
meant — it burst a window in me

I thought nothing could mend.
It all came back to me this morning. That's
why I brought in these twigs — for you.

Taller, Wider

What is it I feel: this odd fusion
of elation and sadness that makes me
stop weeding and stand this way, hands
on hips, knee-deep in lavender?

The air, zealous with aromas
and swirls of bees, lisps in the breeze.
The willow I planted by the pond
five years ago in May, no longer

needs that stake I hammered
deep in dense, moist clay. It sways,
strokes the water with nimble limbs,
and will grow fuller still — taller, wider.

Bouncing off the granite
back of Sainte-Victoire, the dull
timbre of church bells. A quiet noon.
My hands sting with nettles and dirt.

On my wrist, the bracelet
love locked around it, long ago,
on a winter night. A wilted leaf
now caught between its links —

I leave it there: I am learning happiness.

Notes

In "Great Gullet Creek": "Polders" are tracts of lowlands reclaimed from the sea. De Grote Geule is situated northwest of Antwerp, near the estuary of the Scheldt River and on the border between Belgium and Holland. It is surrounded by farmland and potato polders. Lodewijk van Maele, Earl of Flanders, decreed the first dam be built near the Grote Geule in 1353. Since then, generations of Flemish and Dutch poldermannen (polder-men) have been taking land back from the North Sea, and fighting its tides and floods with man-made dams. Since 1972, De Grote Geule is protected and managed by the Belgian Royal Association for Monuments and Nature Preservation. Large numbers of domestic and migrating birds come to nest in De Grote Geule. The small one-room log cabin, built on the creek in the 1940s, still stands.

In the fourth section of the poem, the word "daag" is Flemish for "day" — as in "good-day."

In "Seven Fragments on Hearing a Hammer Pounding": in the section entitled "Antwerp, 1947," the word "Joden" is Dutch for "Jews."

In the section entitled "Give Yourself in Belief," the quote is from Stephen Dobyns.

In "Vase": the last two lines of the poem are my translation from a line in Arthur Rimbaud's poem "Seven-Year-Old Poets." Some images were adapted from the same poem as well as from Rimbaud's "The Sleeper in the Valley."

Acknowledgments

Grateful acknowledgment is made to the editors of the following publications and literary websites in which these works or earlier versions of them previously appeared:

AGNI: "Listener of Bats"

Bloomsbury Review: "Dinner at the Who's Who"

Crazyhorse: "What I feel"

Harvard Review: "The Pleasures of Hating," "Vase"

LUNA: "Bench in Aix-en-Provence"

Maine Times: "Harvard Bridge"

Ohio Review: "Petition to Be Inconsolable"

Ploughshares: "The Rat Trinity"

Tar River: "Letter to a Friend"

Washington Square: "Antwerp, 1947" (from "Seven Fragments on Hearing a Hammer Pounding")

Web Publications

canwehaveourballback: "G.O.D.'s Trucks"

Drought: A Literary Review: "Brier," "Discovering Rhyme," "August City Shadows," "At Dawn"

In Posse Review (WebDelSol.com): "Great Gullet Creek"

In Posse Review Multi-Ethnic Anthology (WebDelSol.com): "Seven Fragments on Hearing a Hammer Pounding"

Samsara: "Belong," "Our Lady of Pity," "Community Garden," "Taller, Wider"

Dedications

"Dinner at the Who's Who" is for Tony Hoagland,

"August City Shadows" is for Aidan O'Brien,

"Great Gullet Creek" for Kristien Hemmerechts,

"The Rat Trinity" is for Doug Goetsch,

"Filthy Savior" is for Kim Addonizio,

"Follen Street" is for Barry and Grace Mazur.

For Kurt: *amour, toujours.*

I'm deeply thankful, Steve Huff, for your heroic patience, unfailing sense of humor and stubborn assurance: this book wouldn't have been completed without your support; and thank you, Thom Ward, for the ear and heart.

Lasting gratitude to the Warren Wilson community of writers.

I'm so lucky to have you as friends: Jake Anderson, Barry Burchell, Doug Goetsch, Kristien Hemmerechts, André Iweins, Meg Kearney, Barry and Grace Mazur, Charles and Helen Simic, Carol Houck Smith, Guy and Lorna Vanparys, and Kelleen Zubick —

and such love for you Maëlle — *ma belle lumière.*

About the Author

Laure-Anne Bosselaar grew up in Belgium and lived throughout Europe and the United States, to which she moved in 1987. Fluent in four languages, she has worked for Belgian and Luxembourgian radio and television stations, was a teacher of French poetry, and published a collection of French poems. She is currently translating contemporary American poetry into French, and Flemish poetry into English. She holds a Master of Fine Arts degree from the Warren Wilson Program for Writers. She lives in Cambridge, Massachusetts, with her husband, poet and editor Kurt Brown, with whom she co-edited *Night Out: Poems about Hotels, Motels, Restaurants and Bars.* She is the editor of *Outsiders: Poems about Rebels, Exiles and Renegades* and of *Urban Nature: Poems about Wildlife in the City.* She teaches poetry workshops at writers' conferences across the country and conducts private workshops in Cambridge.

BOA Editions, LTD.:
American Poets Continuum Series

No. 1   *The Führer Bunker: A Cycle of Poems in Progress*
W.D. Snodgrass

No. 2   *She*
M.L. Rosenthal

No. 3   *Living With Distance*
Ralph J. Mills, Jr.

No. 4   *Not Just Any Death*
Michael Waters

No. 5   *That Was Then: New and Selected Poems*
Isabella Gardner

No. 6   *Things That Happen Where There Aren't Any People*
William Stafford

No. 7   *The Bridge of Change: Poems 1974–1980*
John Logan

No. 8   *Signatures*
Joseph Stroud

No. 9   *People Live Here: Selected Poems 1949–1983*
Louis Simpson

No. 10   *Yin*
Carolyn Kizer

No. 11   *Duhamel: Ideas of Order in Little Canada*
Bill Tremblay

No. 12   *Seeing It Was So*
Anthony Piccione

No. 13   *Hyam Plutzik: The Collected Poems*

No. 14   *Good Woman: Poems and a Memoir 1969–1980*
Lucille Clifton

No. 15   *Next: New Poems*
Lucille Clifton

No. 16   *Roxa: Voices of Culver Family*
William B. Patrick

No. 17   *John Logan: The Collected Poems*

No. 18   *Isabella Gardner: The Collected Poems*

No. 19   *The Sunken Lightship*
Peter Makuck

No. 20   *The City in Which I Love You*
Li-Young Lee

No. 21   *Quilting: Poems 1987–1990*
Lucille Clifton

No. 22   *John Logan: The Collected Fiction*

No. 23   *Shenandoah and Other Verse Plays*
Delmore Schwartz

No. 24   *Nobody Lives on Arthur Godfrey Boulevard*
Gerald Costanzo

No. 25   *The Book of Names: New and Selected Poems*
Barton Sutter

No. 26   *Each in His Season*
W.D. Snodgrass

No. 27   *Wordworks: Poems Selected and New*
Richard Kostelanetz

No. 28   *What We Carry*
Dorianne Laux

No. 29   *Red Suitcase*
Naomi Shihab Nye

No. 30   *Song*
Brigit Pegeen Kelly

No. 31   *The Fuhrer Bunker: The Complete Cycle*
W.D. Snodgrass

No. 32   *For the Kingdom*
Anthony Piccione

No. 33   *The Quicken Tree*
Bill Knott

No. 34   *These Upraised Hands*
William B. Patrick

No. 35   *Crazy Horse in Stillness*
William Heyen

No. 36   *Quick, Now, Always*
         Mark Irwin

No. 37   *I Have Tasted the Apple*
         Mary Crow

No. 38   *The Terrible Stories*
         Lucille Clifton

No. 39   *The Heat of Arrivals*
         Ray Gonzalez

No. 40   *Jimmy & Rita*
         Kim Addonizio

No. 41   *Green Ash, Red Maple, Black
         Gum*
         Michael Waters

No. 42   *Against Distance*
         Peter Makuck

No. 43   *The Night Path*
         Laurie Kutchins

No. 44   *Radiography*
         Bruce Bond

No. 45   *At My Ease: Uncollected Poems
         of the Fifties and Sixties*
         David Ignatow

No. 46   *Trillium*
         Richard Foerster

No. 47   *Fuel*
         Naomi Shihab Nye

No. 48   *Gratitude*
         Sam Hamill

No. 49   *Diana, Charles,
         & the Queen*
         William Heyen

No. 50   *Plus Shipping*
         Bob Hicok

No. 51   *Cabato Sentora*
         Ray Gonzalez

No. 52   *We Didn't Come Here
         for This*
         William B. Patrick
         Introduction by
         Fred Chappell

No. 53   *The Vandals*
         Alan Michael Parker

No. 54   *To Get Here*
         Wendy Mnookin

No. 55   *Living Is What I Wanted:
         Last Poems*
         David Ignatow

No. 56   *Dusty Angel*
         Michael Blumenthal

No. 57   *The Tiger Iris*
         Joan Swift

No. 58   *White City*
         Mark Irwin

No. 59   *Laugh at the End of the World:
         Collected Comic Poems
         1969–1999*
         Bill Knott

No. 60   *Blessing the Boats: New and
         Selected Poems: 1988–2000*
         Lucille Clifton

No. 61   *Tell Me*
         Kim Addonizio

No. 62   *Smoke*
         Dorianne Laux

No. 63   *Parthenopi: New and
         Selected Poems*
         Michael Waters

No. 64   *Rancho Notorious*
         Richard Garcia

No. 65   *Jam*
         Joe-Anne McLaughlin
         Introduction by
         Stephen Dunn

No. 66   *A. Poulin, Jr. Selected Poems*
         Edited with an
         Introduction by Michael
         Waters

No. 67   *Small Gods of Grief*
         Laure-Anne Bosselaar

COLOPHON

The Isabella Gardner Poetry Award is given biennially to a poet in
mid-career whose manuscript is of exceptional merit.
Poet, actress, and associate editor of *Poetry* magazine,
Isabella Gardner (1915–1981) published five celebrated collections
of poetry, was three times nominated for the National Book
Award, and was the first recipient of the New York State
Walt Whitman Citation of Merit for Poetry.
She championed the work of young and gifted poets,
helping many of them find publication.

Small Gods of Grief, poems by Laure-Anne Bosselaar,
the 2001 selection for the Isabella Gardner Poetry Award,
has been set in Legacy, designed by Ronald Arnholm.

The interior was designed by Valerie Brewster,
Scribe Typography, Port Townsend, WA.

The cover and jacket were designed by
Geri McCormick, Rochester, NY.

The cover art, *La digue* by Leon Spilliart, is courtesy of Musees
Royaux des Beaux-Arts de Belgique, Brussels.

Manufacturing was by McNaughton & Gunn, Saline, MI.

The publication of this book was made possible, in part, by the
special support of the following individuals:

Diann Blakely, Jeanne Braham & Sue Mullen
Nancy & Alan Cameros, Dr. William & Shirley Ann Crosby
Susan DeWitt Davie, Peter & Suzanne Durant
Dane & Judy Gordon, Richard Garth & Mimi Hwang
Deb & Kip Hale, Volena Howe
Peter & Robin Hursh, Robert & Willy Hursh
X.J. Kennedy, Louise Klinke
Archie & Pat Kutz, Rosemary & Lew Lloyd
Robert & Dale Mnookin, Boo Poulin
Deborah Ronnen, Peggy Savlov
Jett & Shelley Whitehead, Pat & Michael Wilder
Chris Wilson, Milton Wood